PAPERBACK **PLUS**

Contents

Lensey Namioka

was born in Beijing, China. She emigrated to America, where she attended Radcliffe College and graduated from the University of California, Berkeley.

Namioka has drawn on her Chinese cultural heritage and her husband's Japanese background in writing for young people. *Yang the Youngest and His Terrible Ear* is based on her own experience as a child growing up in a musical family. Namioka discovered that *she* had a terrible ear, so she switched to the oboe, an instrument with fixed pitch. Namioka has two grown daughters. She lives with her husband in Seattle.

Kees de Kiefte

illustrated *Yang the Youngest and His Terrible Ear* by Lensey Namioka. He lives in the Netherlands.